GRRRRRRRR...

PROFESSOR VON VOLT IS A FAMOUS SCIENTIST. HE DESIGNED THIS TIME MACHINE FOR THE STILTON FAMILY: THEIR MISSION IS TO DEFEAT THE PIRATE CATS AND SAVE HISTORY!

ZKII ZIIK

SPEEDRAT

MOLDY MOZZARELLA! THAT'S NOT A CLOUD...

IT'S A QUEZALCOATLUS!

IT'S ENORMOUS!

THIS FOREST GIVES ME THE CREEPS JUST LOOKING AT IT!

Geronimo Stilton

DINOSAURS IN ACTION

PAPERCUTZ™

GRAPHIC NOVELS AVAILABLE FROM

Graphic Novel #1
"The Discovery of America"

Graphic Novel #2
"The Secret of the Sphinx"

Graphic Novel #3
"The Coliseum Con"

Graphic Novel #4
"Following the Trail of Marco Polo"

Graphic Novel #5
"The Great Ice Age"

Graphic Novel #6
"Who Stole The Mona Lisa?"

Graphic Novel #7
"Dinosaurs in Action"

www.papercutz.com

Geronimo Stilton

DINOSAURS IN ACTION

By Geronimo Stilton

New York

DINOSAURS IN ACTION
© EDIZIONI PIEMME 2009 S.p.A.
Tiziano 32, 20145,
Milan, Italy
Geronimo Stilton names, characters and related indicia are copyright, trademark and
exclusive license of Atlantyca S.p.A.

Text by Geronimo Stilton
Editorial coordination by Patrizia Puricelli
Original editing by Daniela Finistauri
Script by Andrea Denegri
Artistic coordination by Roberta Bianchi
Artistic assistance by Tommaso Valsecchi
Graphic Project by Michela Battaglin
Graphics by Marta Lorini
Cover art and color by Flavio Ferron
Interior illustrations by Giuseppe Ferrario and color by Giulia Zaffaroni
Based on an original idea by Elisabetta Dami

© 2011 — for this work in English language by Papercutz.

Original title: Geronimo Stilton Dinosauri in Azione!

Translation by: Nanette McGuinness

www.geronimostilton.com

Lettering and Production by Ortho
Michael Petranek — Associate Editor
Jim Salicrup
Editor-in-Chief

ISBN: 978-1-59707-239-7

Printed in China.

October 2010 by WKT Co. LTD.
3/F Phase 1 Leader Industrial Centre
188 Texaco Road, Tsuen Wan, N.T.
Hong Kong

Distributed by Macmillan.
First Printing

IN NEW MOUSE CITY ON MOUSE ISLAND, NIGHT WAS PASSING **PEACEFULLY.**

DINOSAURS IN ACTION!

NO ONE COULD EVER HAVE IMAGINED THAT JUST BEFORE DAWN...

...SOMETHING ABSOLUTELY UNEXPECTED WOULD HAPPEN...

...ALONG THE DESERTED DOCKS IN THE HARBOR!

>HUMF!<

THUMP

OUCH!

>OOF!< THAT WAS HARD!

HEY! DID YOU GET YOUR DRIVER'S LICENSE OUT OF A FISHY PUFFS BAG?

ALWAYS THE CRITIC! I WONDER WHY YOU'RE NEVER AT THE *HELM*!

THAT ISN'T THE *QUESTION* YOU SHOULD BE ASKING, BUT RATHER...

...WHY HAVEN'T I FED YOU TO THE SHARKS ALREADY!?!

MAYBE BECAUSE I HAVE TO DRIVE, SINCE YOU DON'T HAVE A DRIVER'S LICENSE!

I'M EMPEROR CATARDONE III OF CATATONIA! I DON'T NEED A DRIVER'S LICENSE! AND DON'T SPEAK TO ME IN THAT TONE OF VOICE!

MEOW DOWN*, YOU TWO!

*CALM DOWN.

THE PLAN WAS TO DOCK AT MOUSE ISLAND SECRETLY! BUT YOU KEEP MAKING NOISE!

NO ONE'S SUPPOSED TO KNOW WE'RE HERE ON MOUSE ISLAND!

COME ON! TAKE THE MOUSE MASKS!

I DON'T GET WHAT ALL THIS MYSTERY IS FOR!

WE'RE *CATS*, MICE ARE AFRAID OF US! NOW THAT WE'RE HERE, WE MIGHT SCARE THEM!

RIGHT! LET'S HAVE A LITTLE FUN INSTEAD OF PUTTING ON THESE UGLY MASKS!

>TSK!< HAVE FUN... HAVE YOU FORGOTTEN WHY WE'RE HERE?

NO, NO, OF COURSE NOT... WE'RE HERE TO UM... TO...

TO FIND PROFESSOR PAWS VON VOLT AND DESTROY HIS TIME MACHINE! THAT WAY NO ONE WILL BE ABLE TO BLOCK OUR PLANS!

OUCH!

RIGHT! HOW MANY TIMES DO I HAVE TO TELL YOU?

LET'S GO!

WHERE?

TO OUR FIRST DAY OF WORK... AT THE *RODENT'S GAZETTE!*

7

IN THE MEANTIME, THE DAY HAD BEGUN, AND I ARRIVED AT MY OFFICE...

HEY THERE, GERONIMO!

SORRY, I HAVEN'T INTRODUCED MYSELF YET...MY NAME IS STILTON,

Geronimo Stilton!

I RUN THE RODENT'S GAZETTE, THE MOST FAMOUS PAPER ON MOUSE ISLAND AND...

I WAS JUST *WAITING* FOR YOU!

COULD YOU DO ME A FAVOR AND TAKE YOUR FEET OFF MY DESK?

...I HAVE A BUNGLING COUSIN NAMED **TRAP!**

COME ON, DON'T WHINE! I WAS THINKING ABOUT YOU THIS MORNING!

ME? HOW NICE... BU[T] WHY?

BECAUSE I WANTED A NICE BREAKFAST AND I KNEW YOU'D TREAT ME!

OH, THAT'S WHY! I THOUGHT SO...

HOW COME IT'S ALWAYS MY TREAT?

WELL, 'CAUSE YOU CAN OFFER ME SOME TEA, AND I CAN OFFER THEE SOME ME!

HMM... OKAY, BUT YOU'LL HAVE TO WAIT... I HAVE SOME URGENT WORK I HAVE TO GET DONE!

OF COURSE! JUST SIGN YOUR PAPERS! WHILE I'M WAITING, I'LL WATCH YOU AND HAVE A FEW LAUGHS!

LAUGHS? WHAT'S THERE TO LAUGH ABOUT IN MY WORK?

OH, IN YOUR WORK, NOTHING...

...BUT YOUR PEN CRACKS ME UP! WHISKERFULS OF LAUGHTER!

SPLASH

>OOF!< I SHOULD'VE EXPECTED A TRICK!

HA, HA! YOU'RE A REAL HOOT, COUSIN!

AHEM... RIGHT! THAT'S REALLY FUNNY...

DR. STILTON? MAY WE COME IN?

WE'RE THE NEW REPORTERS YOUR GRANDFATHER, WILLIAM SHORTPAWS, HIRED! MY NAME IS SPARKLE AND THESE ARE MY ASSISTANTS: SPORTS COMMENTATOR CARLO BIGCAT AND PHOTO JOURNALIST BONZO FLASH!

HERE WE ARE! EVER AT THE READY!

HUNTING FOR SCOOPS!

NEW JOURNALISTS?!?

REALLY... MY GRAND-FATHER SAID NOTHING TO ME...

MAYBE HE FORGOT...

WELL, WE'RE AGGRESSIVE REPORTERS, OR BETTER STILL... PIRATICAL!

RIGHT! HEH, HEH, HEH! HEE, HEE, HEE!

HUH, YES! REAL PIRATES... OUCH!

WHAT AN IDIOT! HE'S GOING TO LET THE CAT OUT OF THE BAG!

THUMP

OW, OW!

UM, RIGHT...WE'RE NEWS PIRATES AND WE CAN'T WAIT TO GET STARTED!

?!?

IN FACT, WE HAVE TO DASH OFF... DUTY CALLS!

WHY ARE WE LEAVING, NOW THAT WE'VE GOT THE RODENT IN OUR PAWS?

RIGHT, WE COULD'VE TAKEN ADVANTAGE OF THE MOMENT AND NABBED HIM...

MEOW DOWN*! WE'LL SWING INTO ACTION WHEN THE TIME IS RIGHT!

*CALM DOWN

HMM... DIDN'T THOSE THREE REPORTERS SEEM A LITTLE STRANGE TO YOU?

ALL I KNOW IS THAT WE'RE LATE FOR BREAKFAST!

OKAY, I GET IT! GIVE ME A COUPLE OF MINUTES TO GET READY!

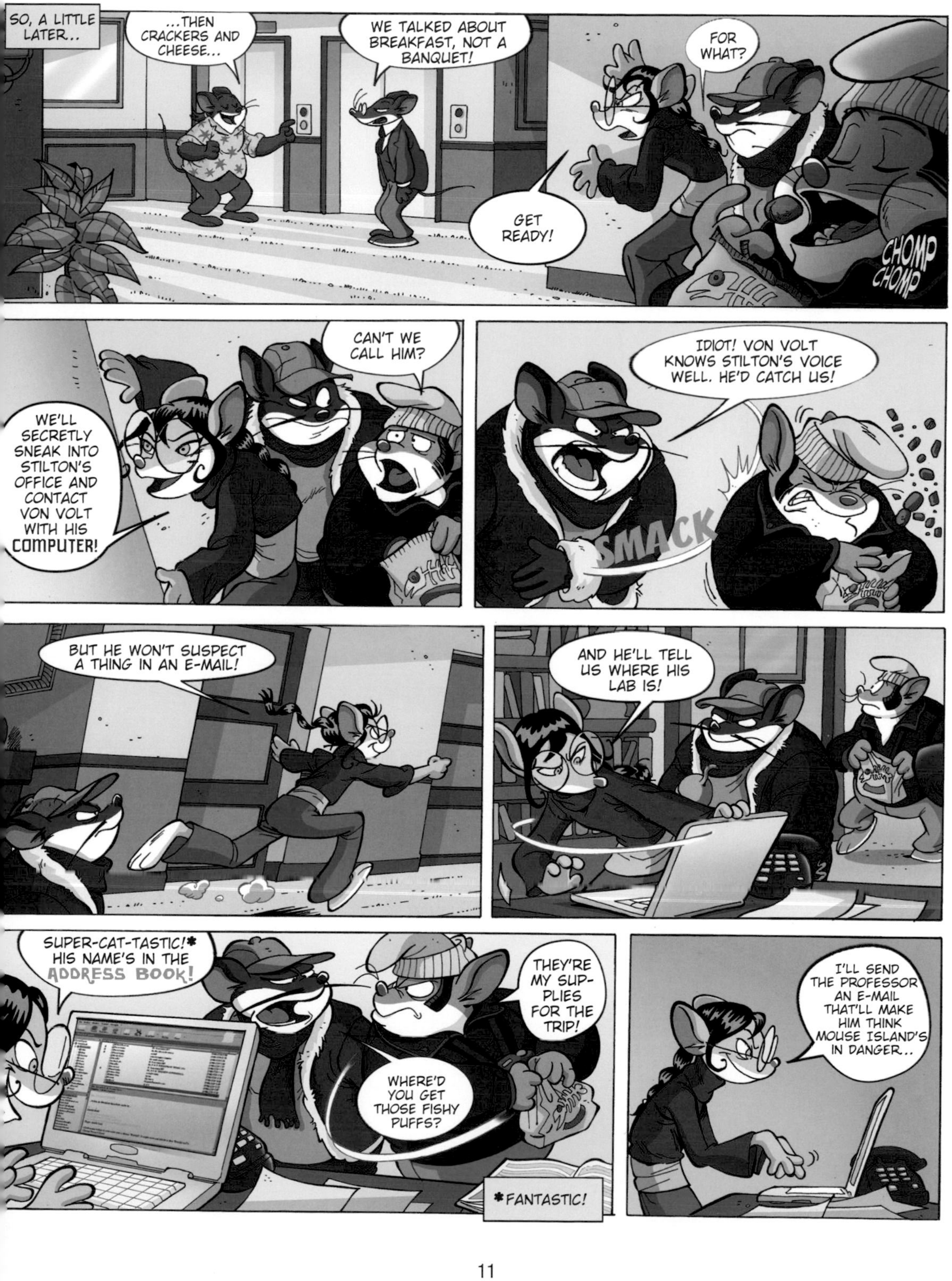

SO, A LITTLE LATER...
...THEN CRACKERS AND CHEESE...
WE TALKED ABOUT BREAKFAST, NOT A BANQUET!
FOR WHAT?
GET READY!
CHOMP CHOMP
CAN'T WE CALL HIM?
WE'LL SECRETLY SNEAK INTO STILTON'S OFFICE AND CONTACT VON VOLT WITH HIS COMPUTER!
IDIOT! VON VOLT KNOWS STILTON'S VOICE WELL. HE'D CATCH US!
SMACK
BUT HE WON'T SUSPECT A THING IN AN E-MAIL!
AND HE'LL TELL US WHERE HIS LAB IS!
SUPER-CAT-TASTIC!* HIS NAME'S IN THE ADDRESS BOOK!
THEY'RE MY SUPPLIES FOR THE TRIP!
WHERE'D YOU GET THOSE FISHY PUFFS?
*FANTASTIC!
I'LL SEND THE PROFESSOR AN E-MAIL THAT'LL MAKE HIM THINK MOUSE ISLAND'S IN DANGER...

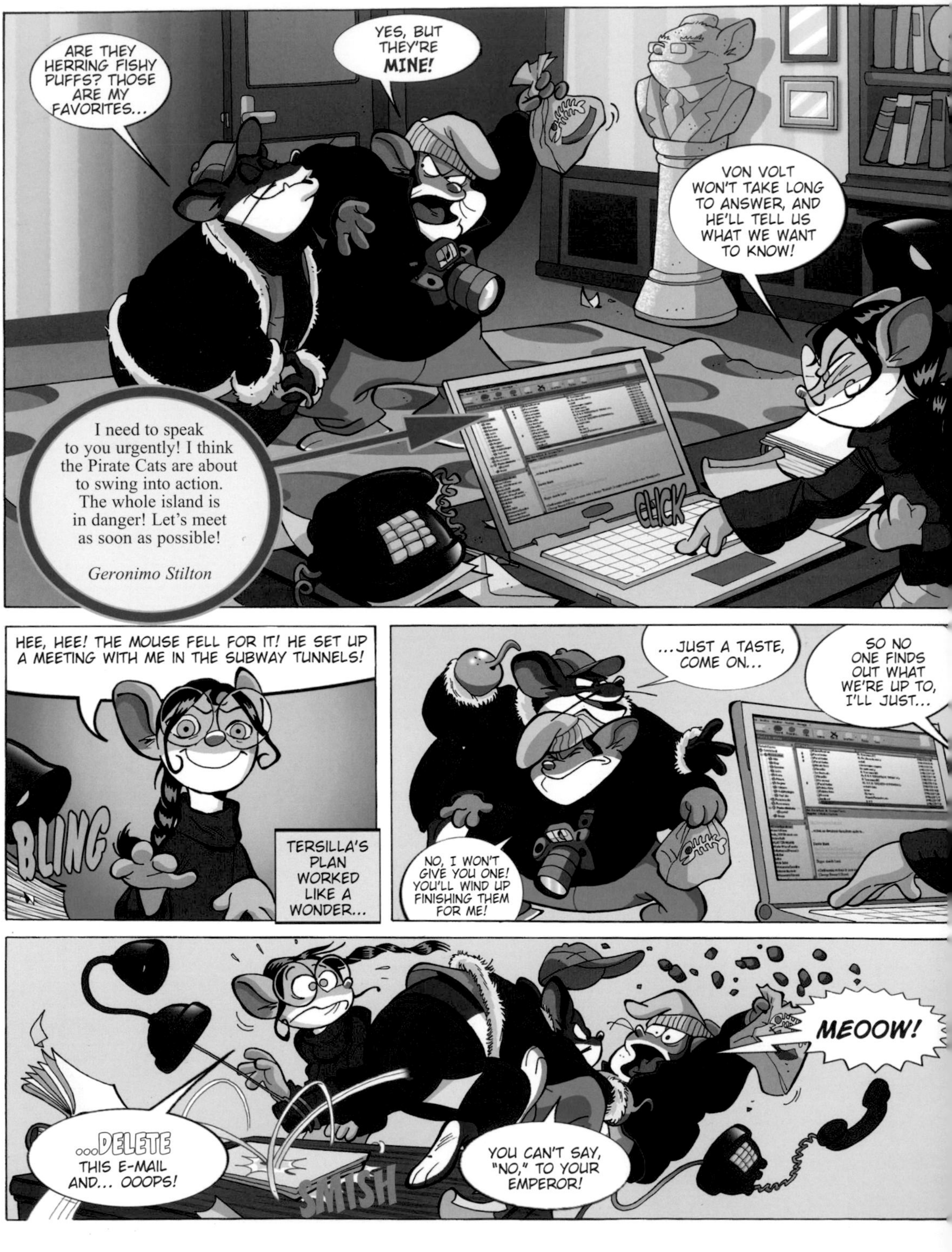
ARE THEY HERRING FISHY PUFFS? THOSE ARE MY FAVORITES...
YES, BUT THEY'RE MINE!
VON VOLT WON'T TAKE LONG TO ANSWER, AND HE'LL TELL US WHAT WE WANT TO KNOW!
I need to speak to you urgently! I think the Pirate Cats are about to swing into action. The whole island is in danger! Let's meet as soon as possible!
Geronimo Stilton
CLICK
HEE, HEE! THE MOUSE FELL FOR IT! HE SET UP A MEETING WITH ME IN THE SUBWAY TUNNELS!
BLING
TERSILLA'S PLAN WORKED LIKE A WONDER...
...JUST A TASTE, COME ON...
SO NO ONE FINDS OUT WHAT WE'RE UP TO, I'LL JUST...
NO, I WON'T GIVE YOU ONE! YOU'LL WIND UP FINISHING THEM FOR ME!
MEOOW!
...DELETE THIS E-MAIL AND... OOOPS!
SMISH
YOU CAN'T SAY, "NO," TO YOUR EMPEROR!

YOU TURNED OFF THE LAPTOP BEFORE I COULD DELETE THE E-MAIL!

NOW I HAVE TO REBOOT IT SO I DON'T LEAVE ANY EVIDENCE!

?!?

HEY, YOU!

WHAT'RE YOU DOING HERE IN UNCLE GERONIMO'S OFFICE?

AND... WHO ARE YOU?

THE KIDS'VE DISCOVERED US AND STILTON MAY BE COMING BACK! LET'S GO!

>GULP!<

?!?

GANGWAY!

HURRY! WE'LL GET OUT THIS WAY!

ONCE I FIND PROFESSOR VON VOLT, NO ONE WILL BE ABLE TO STOP ME!

HEY! LOOK AT THOSE NEW REPORTERS RUN!

THEY MUST BE CHASING AFTER A SCOOP!

QUICK! TO THE SUBWAY!

CAN'T WE TAKE A TAXI?

NO! THE SUBWAY TUNNELS ARE WHERE WE'LL FIND PROFESSOR VON VOLT!

HE SHOULD BE HERE! COME ON, FOLLOW ME!

DO NOT ENTER.

BUT IT SAYS, "DO NOT ENTER"!

IT MUST BE A SECRET PASSAGE!

>GULP!<

SEEMS LIKE IT'S AN ELEVATOR... BUT THERE'S NO BUTTONS!

BUT THEN THAT MEANS WE CAN'T GET OUT...

NO, BUT WE CAN GO DOWN! >GULP!<

VRRRRRRRR

AAAH!

>GULP!< AND WHO ARE YOU?

WUMP

>OOOF!<

FINALLY WE MEET, PROFESSOR!

WE...

...ARE...

...THE PIRATE CATS!

YOU! SCOUNDRELS... WHAT DO YOU WANT FROM ME?

WE CAME TO TAKE YOU ON A LITTLE TRIP...

...WITH A ONE WAY TICKET! HEE, HEE!

WH-WHERE ARE YOU GOING TO TAKE ME?

140 MILLION YEARS AWAY!

WE'RE GOING TO THE CRETACEOUS PERIOD! WHERE YOU WON'T BE ABLE TO BUMP INTO ANYTHING BESIDES DINOSAURS!

THE CRETACEOUS PERIOD

THE THIRD AND LAST PERIOD OF THE MESOZOIC ERA (AFTER THE TRIASSIC AND JURASSIC) BEGAN 140 MILLION YEARS AGO. DURING THIS PERIOD, THE CONTINENTAL MASSES BROKE APART AND STARTED BECOMING THE SHAPE THEY ARE TODAY. MANY MOUNTAIN RANGES FORMED AS A RESULT OF THIS MOVEMENT AND THE INTENSE VOLCANIC ACTIVITY.

In the past so dark and bleak, he'll be stuck for many a week! Hee, hee!

140 million years: a very nice trip, without any tears!

I DON'T WANT TO BE TRAPPED IN PREHISTORY!

WE'LL SEE IF YOU CAN STOP US FROM SCAMPERING THROUGH TIME AGAIN WHEN YOU'RE BACK THERE!

I'VE GOT TO LEAVE A CLUE... AND HOPE SOMEONE WILL FIND IT AND COME RESCUE ME!

CLACK CLACK

BUT IT'S TIME TO STOP WASTING TIME!

PACK HIM UP!

RIGHT AWAY, TERSILLA! HA, HA, HA!

THE CORD HIDDEN IN MY FAKE CAMERA IS PERFECT!

WE'RE READY FOR A LITTLE TRIP!

ANYBODY, HELP!!

BEEP

140000000

BAD **NEWS**, UNCLE GERONIMO!

WE STOPPED BY TO SAY HELLO AND STARTLED THREE SUSPICIOUS-LOOKING GUYS IN YOUR OFFICE!

HI, KIDS! HOW COME YOU'RE HERE?

THE NEW REPORTERS! THAT'S WHY THEY WERE RUNNING!

I DIDN'T LIKE THOSE THREE FROM THE VERY START!

IT LOOKED LIKE THEY WERE INTERESTED IN YOUR COMPUTER!

ACTUALLY, THEY WERE LOGGED ONTO IT, BUT NOW IT'S OFF.

WHEN THEY SAW US, THEY RAN OFF IN A BIG HURRY!

>SNIFF< ...THE STINK OF FISH!

HMM... WHERE THERE'S THE **STINK OF FISH**, THERE'S THE STINK OF THE PIRATE CATS!

BUT WHAT WERE THEY LOOKING FOR?

PERHAPS WE'LL FIND OUT IF WE TURN ON THE COMPUTER!

THERE'S A MESSAGE FROM PROFESSOR VON VOLT!

RIGHT, AND IT'S THE ANSWER TO AN E-MAIL I NEVER SENT!

SOMEONE MUST'VE PASSED THEMSELVES OFF AS YOU!

THIS IS THE WORK OF THE CATS!

LET'S GO! THE CATS HAVE FOUND OUT WHERE THE LAB IS! THE PROFESSOR'S IN DANGER NOW!

BY FOLLOWING THE DIRECTIONS IN THE E-MAIL, WE FOUND PROFESSOR VON VOLT'S LAB!

PROFESSOR VON VOLT!

THERE'S NO ONE HERE!

OOOPS!

WUMP

>SIGH!< WE GOT HERE TOO LATE, KIDS!

UNCLE TRAP, WHAT'S THAT?

OW, OW!

HUH! WHAT? WHERE?

>BLEH!< WHAT A STENCH!

THERE'S NO LONGER ANY DOUBT! THE CATS CAME THROUGH HERE AND KIDNAPPED PROFESSOR VON VOLT!

HERRING FISHY PUFFS! I LANDED ON THEM!

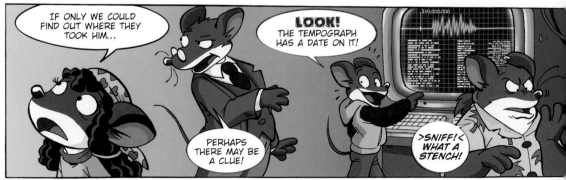

IF ONLY WE COULD FIND OUT WHERE THEY TOOK HIM...

LOOK! THE TEMPOGRAPH HAS A DATE ON IT!

PERHAPS THERE MAY BE A CLUE!

>SNIFF!< WHAT A STENCH!

140 MILLION YEARS! WHY'D THE PROFESSOR PUT THAT DATE ON THE TEMPOGRAPH?

MAYBE THAT'S JUST THE **CLUE** WE'RE LOOKING FOR!

140.000.000

OR MAYBE IT'S THE AMOUNT OF TIME IT'LL TAKE TO GET THIS STINK OFF MY PAWS! >BLEHH!<

I THINK THE PROFESSOR WANTED TO TELL US HOW TO FIND HIM AND RESCUE HIM!

SO THE PROFESSOR'S IN PREHISTO-RY?

MAYBE THE CATS WANTED TO DUMP HIM IN A TIME HE COULDN'T GET BACK FROM!

POOR PROFESSOR VON VOLT WILL FIND HIMSELF ALL ALONE IN THE MIDDLE OF dinosaurs!

...WITHOUT EVEN A BITE OF PARMESAN TO NIBBLE ON! >SIGH!<

WE HAVE TO GO GET HIM OURSELVES! WHEN A **FRIEND** NEEDS HELP, YOU CAN'T SIT IDLY BY!

AND HE WON'T BE ABLE TO GET BACK TO THE PRESENT AGAIN!

RAT-TASTIC!

YOU'RE THE GREATEST, UNCLE G!

LET'S TAKE A TRIP TO THE PAST AND HOPE WE FIND PROFESSOR VON VOLT!

YOU'RE RIGHT, WE CAN'T GO BACK, BUT... WE DON'T KNOW ANYTHING ABOUT **PREHISTORY!**

...AND THIS TIME, THE PROFESSOR ISN'T AROUND TO GIVE US INFORMATION THAT CAN HELP US OUT!

BUT I KNOW WHO CAN GIVE US A HAND!

MY FRIEND AND PALEONTOLOGIST... KAREN VON FOSSILS! SHE'S THE DIRECTOR OF THE NEW MOUSE CITY NATURAL HISTORY MUSEUM AND A DINOSAUR EXPERT!

Karen Von Fossils

"KAREN WAS EXCITED AND CAME RIGHT AWAY!"

I'M SO GLAD I CAN HELP YOU...

...PLUS I'VE ALWAYS WANTED TO VISIT PREHISTORY!

140,000.00

THEN GET YOURSELF READY FOR THE TRIP OF YOUR DREAMS!

PROFESSOR VON VOLT ALREADY SET OUR DESTINATION TIME!

START UP THE SPEEDRAT!

WITH PLEASURE!

THAT'S THE TAKEOFF BUT- TON...WILL YOU US THE HONOR DOCTOR VON FOSSILS?

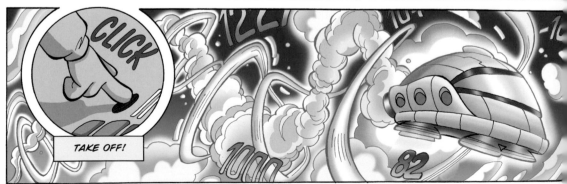

CLICK

TAKE OFF!

20

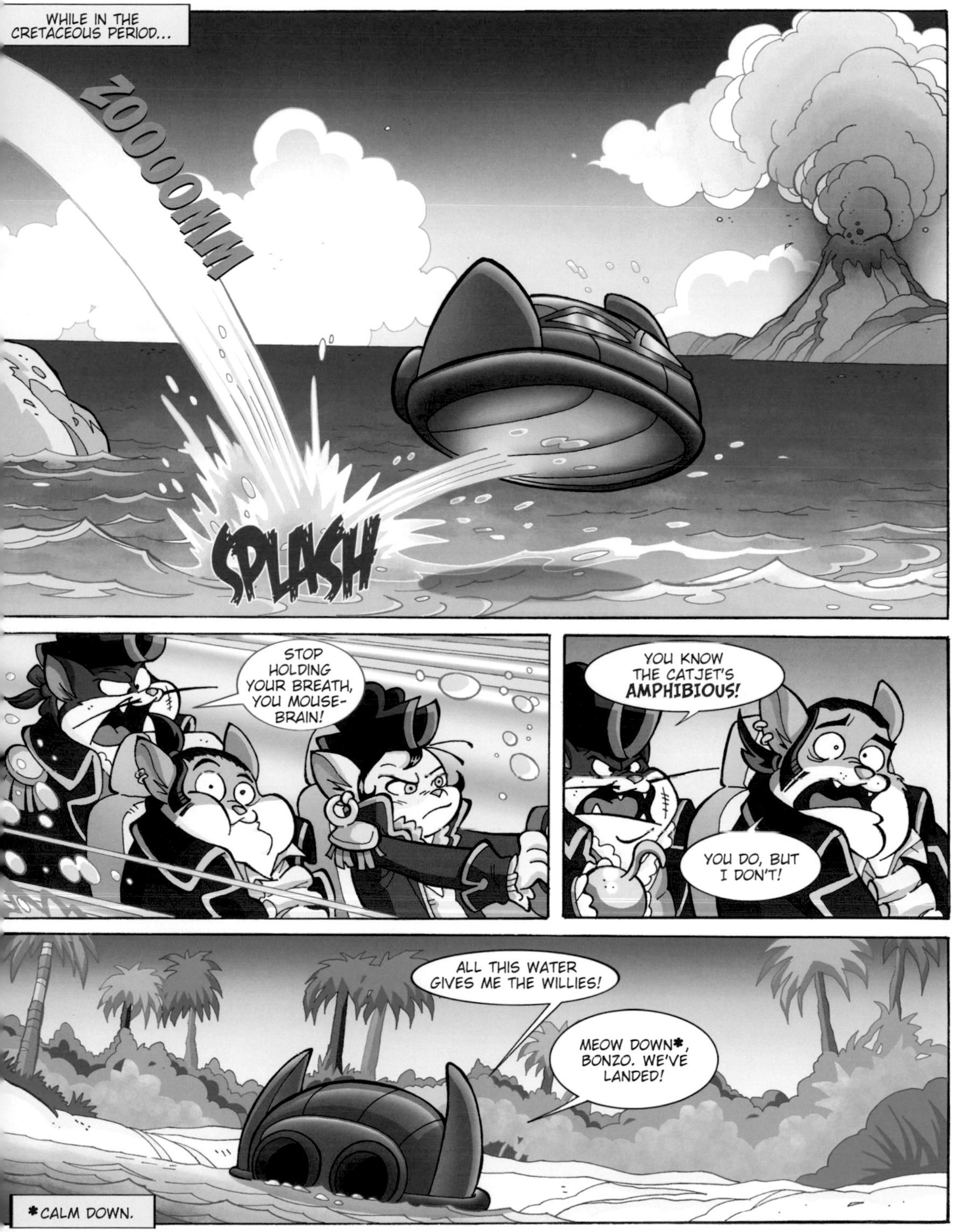
WHILE IN THE CRETACEOUS PERIOD...
ZOOOOMM
SPLASH
STOP HOLDING YOUR BREATH, YOU MOUSE-BRAIN!
YOU KNOW THE CATJET'S AMPHIBIOUS!
YOU DO, BUT I DON'T!
ALL THIS WATER GIVES ME THE WILLIES!
MEOW DOWN*, BONZO. WE'VE LANDED!
*CALM DOWN.

I HOPE YOU LIKE IT HERE, PROFESSOR, BECAUSE YOU'RE GOING TO BE STAYING A VERY LONG, LONG TIME!

WELCOME TO THE CRETACEOUS PERIOD!

HELP! LET GO OF ME!

AS YOU WISH, PROFESSOR!

OUCH!

THUMP

NO! I DON'T WANT TO STAY HERE! PULL ME BACK UP!

GLADLY, RIGHT AWAY!

HEE, HEE! IT'S LIKE A YO-YO!

CRASH

STOP PLAYING AROUND!

?!?

COME ON, DITCH THE MOUSE AND LET'S LEAVE!

DID YOU SEE WHAT I SAW?

YES!!!

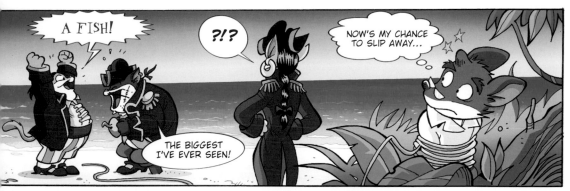

A FISH!

THE BIGGEST I'VE EVER SEEN!

?!?

NOW'S MY CHANCE TO SLIP AWAY...

...BEFORE THOSE NASTY CATS FEED ME TO THE FISH!

WE NEED A FISHING POLE!

FIRE UP THE COALS!

WHAT'RE YOU THINKING OF, YOU FATHEADS?

WHICH MEANS: A HUGE FEAST!

THAT FISH IS HUGE!

BUT... THAT'S A PREHISTORIC ANIMAL!

SO IT IS! AND WE'LL BE THE FIRST CATS IN THE WORLD TO HAVE THE MOST MEMORABLE PIG-OUT IN HISTORY!

MORE THAN THAT... IN PREHISTORY!

PLOTOSAURUS

THE NAME OF THIS AQUATIC REPTILE THAT LIVED IN THE CRETACEOUS MEANS "FLOATING LIZARD." WITH A LENGTH OF UP TO AROUND 42 FEET, IT HAD A TAPERED BODY, THE END OF ITS TAIL WAS IN THE SHAPE OF A RHOMBUS, AND IT HAD LARGE EYES THAT GAVE IT EXCELLENT UNDERWATER VISION.

B-BUT... WE NEED TO LEAVE AND FINISH OUR MISSION!

YUM! MY MOUTH IS WATERING!

THIS LONG STICK WILL DO THE JOB FOR US!

CRACK

DO WHAT YOU WANT... BUT, JUST SO YOU KNOW, PROFESSOR VON VOLT HAS ALREADY RUN OFF!

WHA-!

YEAH, HE'S GOING TO BE STUCK HERE, JUST AS WE PLANNED!

INSTEAD LET'S THINK...

BAH! WHO CARES ABOUT THAT MOUSE NOW?

SWISS

I SEE IT! I SEE IT! CAST THE BAIT!

...ABOUT GETTING OURSELVES AN AFTERNOON SNACK!

>GROAN!< I SMELL THE STINK OF TROUBLE!

24

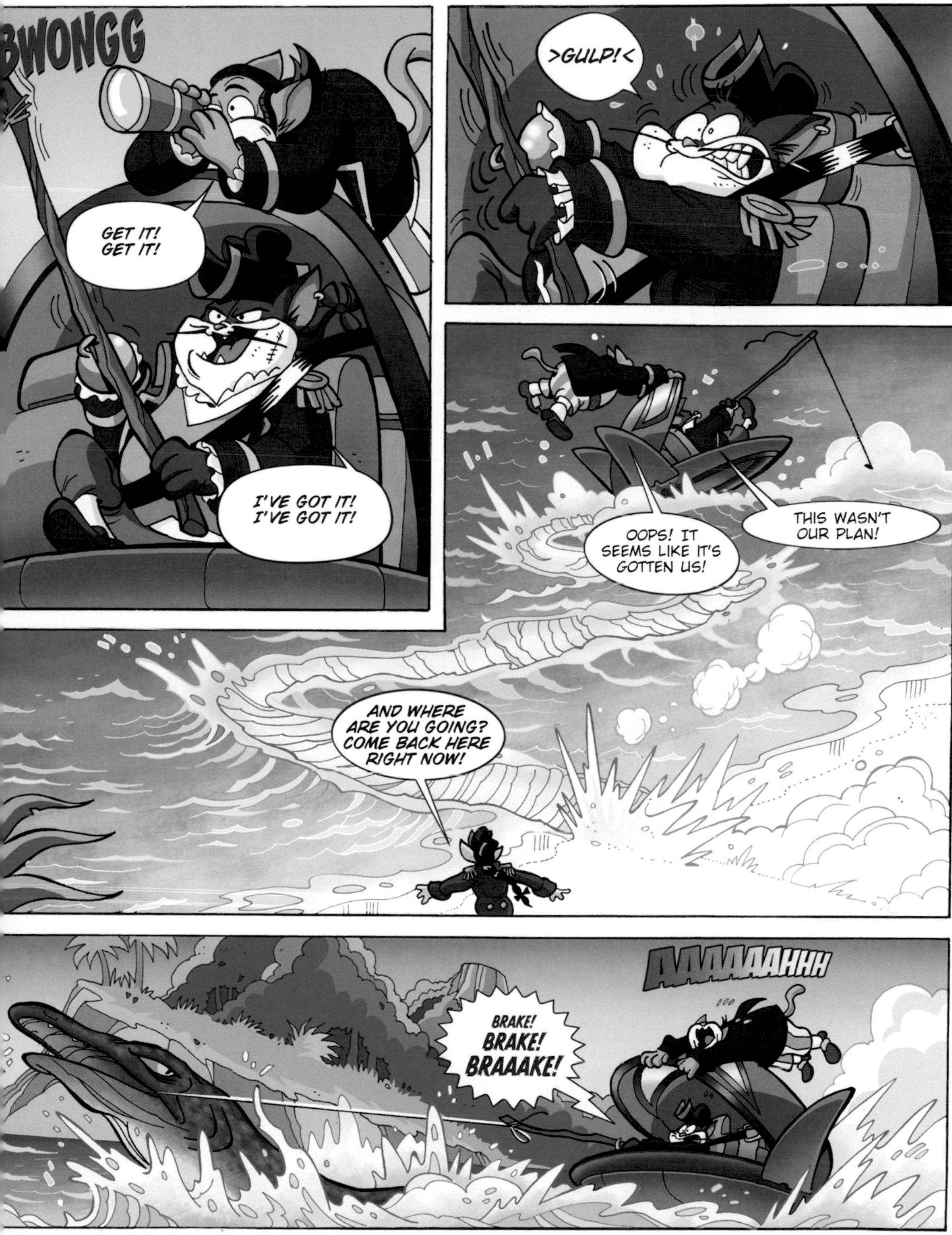
BWONGG
GET IT! GET IT!
I'VE GOT IT! I'VE GOT IT!
>GULP!<
OOPS! IT SEEMS LIKE IT'S GOTTEN US!
THIS WASN'T OUR PLAN!
AND WHERE ARE YOU GOING? COME BACK HERE RIGHT NOW!
AAAAAAHHH
BRAKE! BRAKE! BRAAAKE!

MEANWHILE...

...THE SPEEDRAT...

...HAS LANDED NEAR THE BAY!

UNCLE G, LOOK AT ALL THESE Flowers!

AND FEEL HOW HOT IT IS!

FLOWERS

DURING THE CRETACEOUS PERIOD, FLOWERS LIKE WATER LILIES AND MAGNOLIAS APPEARED FOR THE FIRST TIME. THESE PLANTS MULTIPLIED RAPIDLY, THANKS TO THE INSECTS THAT CAME NEAR THEM, ATTRACTED BY THE COLOR AND SCENT OF THE FLOWERS, TRANSPORTING THEIR POLLEN, AND HELPING MORE PLANTS TO GROW.

IN THIS ER THE CLIMATE WAS HOT AN HUMID OVER THE WHOLE PLANET, AND THERE STARTED TO BE DISTINCT SEASONS.

WELL, NOW IT SEEMS LIKE IT'S CLOUDING OVER

MOLDY MOZZARELLA! THAT'S NOT A CLOUD...

IT'S A QUEZALCOATLUS!

IT'S ENORMOUS!

AND IT'S LOOKING FOR PREY... IT'S HEADING FOR US!

HIDE!

LOOK! IT'S GOING AWAY!

THANK GOODNESS... I WOULDN'T HAVE WANTED TO WIND UP IN ITS BELLY!

WE WERE LUCKY! THE QUEZALCOATLUS IS THE BIGGEST FLYING ANIMAL THAT EVER LIVED.

UNCLE G! THERE ARE **TRACKS** IN THE SAND!

THE CATJET WAS HERE, NO DOUBT ABOUT IT!

LOOK! THERE ARE SOME PRINTS THAT GO TOWARDS THOSE PALM TREES!

IT SEEMS LIKE THE CAT'S SHIP WAS DRAGGED INTO THE WATER!

THERE'RE ALSO SOME TRACKS BETWEEN THESE BUSHES!

THEY HEAD TOWARDS THAT FOREST OF **SEQUOIAS**!

PLANTS AND FLOWERS

IN THE CRETACEOUS PERIOD, IN ADDITION TO THE TREE FERNS THAT HAD ALREADY APPEARED IN THE JURASSIC PERIOD, THERE WERE ALSO THE ANCESTORS OF MODERN PALM TREES, AS WELL AS THE FIRST SEQUOIAS. SEQUOIA LEAVES WERE GREATLY PRIZED BY THE LARGE HERBIVOROUS DINOSAURS. SEQUOIA TREES HAVE SURVIVED TO TODAY.

LET'S SPLIT UP AND FOLLOW THE TRACKS! WE MUST FIND PROFESSOR VON VOLT!

RIGHT! ON YOUR PAWS, COUSIN! YOU AND I'LL GO THAT WAY!

>OOF!< SPLIT UP?

THIS FOREST GIVES ME THE *CREEPS* JUST LOOKING AT IT!

NOT TO MENTION THAT THERE ARE SCARY CREATURES EVERYWHERE!

DON'T WORRY, SCAREDY-MOUSE! I'LL ALWAYS BE RIGHT WITH YOU!

I DON'T KNOW WHY, BUT THAT DOESN'T REASSURE ME!

YOU UNDERESTIMATE ME! I KNOW A LOT OF THINGS ABOUT PREHISTORIC ANIMALS!

THEN YOU KNOW WHY THEY'RE CALLED **DINOSAURS...?**

WELL, NO! BECAUSE I'D RATHER NOT CALL THEM AT ALL... I'M MUCH HAPPIER IF THEY STAY AWAY!

HA, HA!

SIR RICHARD OWEN (1804-1892)

WAS AN ENGLISH PALEONTOLOGIST. IN 1841, HE COLLECTED SOME PREHISTORIC BONES THAT HAD BEEN FOUND IN HIS LIFETIME AND, AFTER STUDYING THEM, CLASSIFIED THE STRANGE ANIMALS THAT THEY BELONGED TO UNDER THE NAME OF "DINOSAURIA," WHICH MEANS "TERRIBLE LIZARD." THIS LABEL IS WHERE THE TERM "DINOSAURS" COMES FROM.

AND TO THINK WE'RE THE FIRST EVER TO OBSERVE THESE CREATURES UP CLOSE!

THAT'S TRUE... NO ONE HAS EVER ENCOUNTERED THEM BEFORE!

WE'LL BE ABLE TO SEE THINGS NOBODY'S EVER SEEN!

EXACTLY RIGHT! EVERYTHING WE KNOW ABOUT DINOSAURS WE'VE LEARNED FROM STUDYING THEIR FOSSILS!

ONE THING'S FOR SURE, THOUGH...

HOW FOSSILS ARE FORMED

WHAT PALEONTOLOGISTS KNOW ABOUT DINOSAURS COMES FROM STUDYING THE FOSSILS THAT HAVE BEEN UNCOVERED. FOSSILS ARE THE REMAINS OF PLANTS AND ANIMALS THAT HAVE BEEN PRESERVED UNTIL OUR DAY. THIS PROCESS OF PRESERVATION, WHICH IS CALLED "MINERALIZATION," COULD ONLY TAKE PLACE IN CERTAIN SITUATIONS, FOR EXAMPLE, WHEN THE BODY OF A DEAD DINOSAUR WAS NEAR A RIVER OR A LAKE, OR HAD BEEN CARRIED TO THE SEA AND SANK TO THE BOTTOM. IN THAT CASE, THE BOTTOM OF THE SEA WAS COVERED BY DIRT AND OTHER SEDIMENTS THAT SLOWED DOWN THE DECOMPOSITION OF THE BODY. AT THIS POINT, DUE TO VARIOUS CHEMICAL REACTIONS, THE ORGANIC SUBSTANCE IN THE BODY WAS TRANSFORMED INTO MINERAL MATTER. SO FOSSILS ARE THE REMAINS OF ANIMALS OR PLANTS THAT DIDN'T DISAPPEAR BECAUSE THEY WERE TRANSFORMED INTO ROCKS OVER TIME. DUE TO THIS TRANSFORMATION, WE CANNOT REPRODUCE SOME OF THE CHARACTERISTICS OF THESE ANCIENT LIVING BEINGS, SUCH AS, FOR EXAMPLE, THEIR COLOR. IN ADDITION, SCHOLARS HAVEN'T ALWAYS RECONSTRUCTED THE MINERALIZED REMAINS OF DINOSAURS IN THE RIGHT WAY, WHICH HAS SOMETIMES LED TO MISTAKES IN ASSEMBLING THEIR SKELETONS.

A LOT OF DINOSAURS WERE HUGE AND **SCARY!**

RIGHT, EVEN BIGGER THAN MY HOUSE!

NOW LET'S GET GOING! PROFESSOR VON VOLT MAY NEED US!

YES, WE HAVE TO FIND HIM AS SOON AS POSSIBLE!

AS WE'D AGREED, WE SPLIT UP...

HEY, GERONIMO, LOOK OUT FOR THAT BRANCH!

WHAT BRANCH?

THAT BRANCH!

OUCH!

IF YOU ONLY THINK ABOUT FOLLOWING THE TRACKS AND ALWAYS KEEP YOUR EYES GLUED TO THE GROUND...

...YOU REALLY RUN THE RISK OF WINDING UP IN...

...HOT WATER!

HELP!

MOLDY MOZZARELLA!

YOW!

THIS PIT SHOULDN'T BE HERE! SOMEONE COULD FALL IN AND BRUISE THEIR TAILBONE!

JUST LIKE WE DID...

>GULP!< I HOPE I'M WRONG, BUT THIS DOESN'T SEEM TO BE A NORMAL PIT!

?!?

LOOK! WE FELL RIGHT INTO THE TRACK OF A DINOSAUR!

>GULP!< YOU'RE RIGHT... IT'S REALLY HUGE!

IT'S GOT TO BE A TITANOSAUR! READ SOMEWHERE THAT IT'S ONL OF THE BIGGEST TERRESTRIAL DINOSAURS THAT EVER EXISTED!

THE TITANOSAUR

WAS A HERBIVOROUS DINOSAUR THAT LIVED IN THE CRETACEOUS PERIOD. IT COULD REACH A LENGTH OF 49 FEET AND A WEIGHT OF 20 TONS. ITS ELONGATED, FLEXIBLE NECK ENDED IN A TINY HEAD AND ITS MASSIVE BODY WAS SUPPORTED BY SQUAT LEGS LIKE THOSE OF AN ELEPHANT. A ROW OF BONY PLATES RAN ALONG ITS BACK.

DON'T GET STRESSED OUT, COUSIN!... MAYBE IT WAS JUST A LIZARD WITH SLIGHTLY SWOLLEN FEET THAT PASSED THROUGH HERE!

LET'S GRAB ONTO THIS BRANCH AND TRY TO GET OUT OF HERE!

BRANCH? ODD, I DIDN'T SEE THAT BEFORE!

GRRRRRRR

DID YOU SAY SOMETHING, GERONIMO?

UM, NO! I THOUGHT THAT WAS YOUR **STOMACH!**

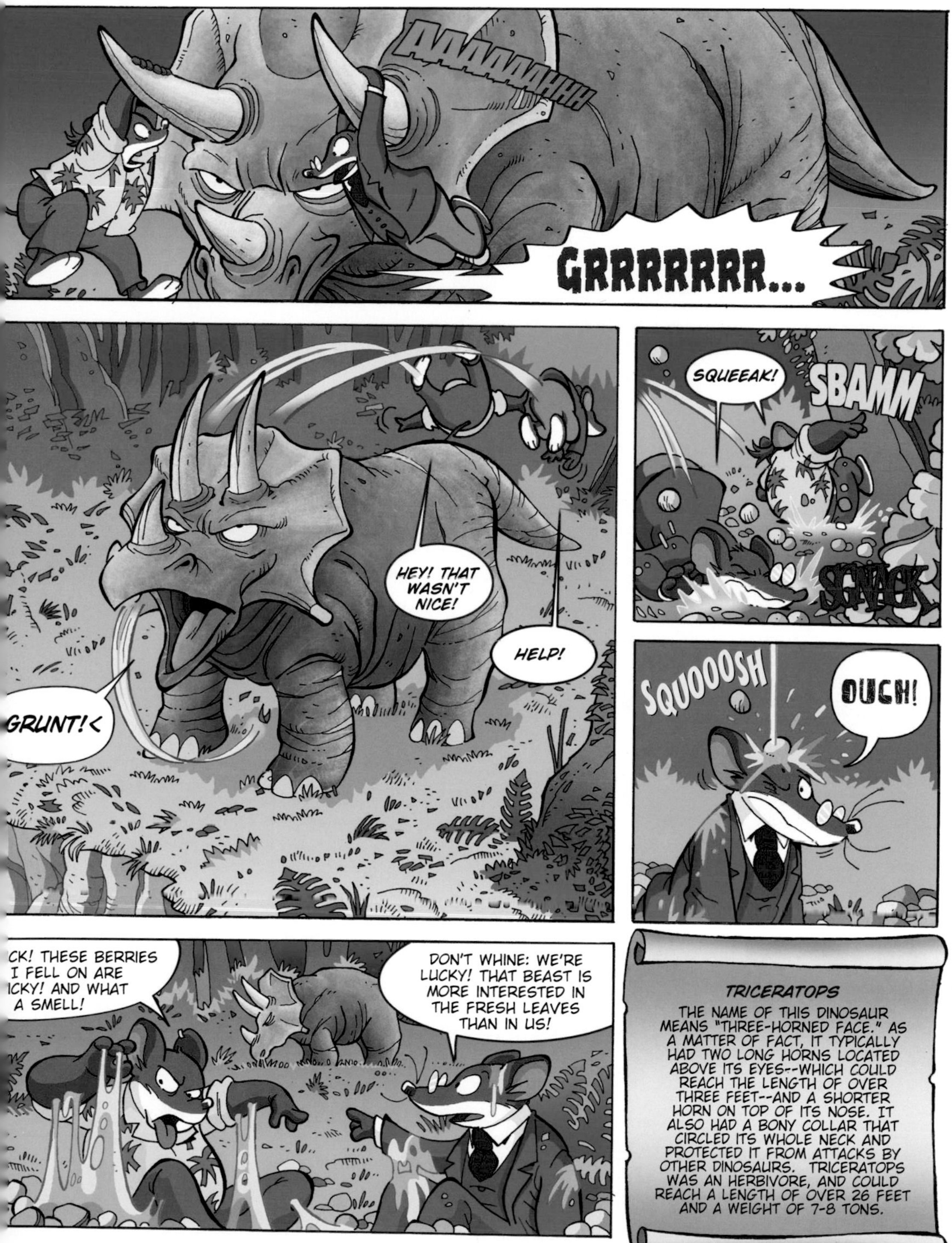
AAAAAAAHHH
GRRRRRRR...
HEY! THAT WASN'T NICE!
HELP!
GRUNT!<
SQUEEAK!
SBAMM
SGNACK
SQUOOOSH
OUCH!
CK! THESE BERRIES I FELL ON ARE ICKY! AND WHAT A SMELL!
DON'T WHINE: WE'RE LUCKY! THAT BEAST IS MORE INTERESTED IN THE FRESH LEAVES THAN IN US!
TRICERATOPS
THE NAME OF THIS DINOSAUR MEANS "THREE-HORNED FACE." AS A MATTER OF FACT, IT TYPICALLY HAD TWO LONG HORNS LOCATED ABOVE ITS EYES--WHICH COULD REACH THE LENGTH OF OVER THREE FEET--AND A SHORTER HORN ON TOP OF ITS NOSE. IT ALSO HAD A BONY COLLAR THAT CIRCLED ITS WHOLE NECK AND PROTECTED IT FROM ATTACKS BY OTHER DINOSAURS. TRICERATOPS WAS AN HERBIVORE, AND COULD REACH A LENGTH OF OVER 26 FEET AND A WEIGHT OF 7-8 TONS.

THAT'S SCARY! I'M shaking LIKE A BOWL OF RICOTTA PUDDING!

I CAN WELL BELIEVE IT!

!!!

TAKING A STROLL AROUND HERE CAN LEAD TO NASTY ENCOUNTERS!

>OOF!<

>GULP!< A TALKING FERN IS REALLY TOO MUCH!

CALM DOWN, TRAP! DON'T YOU RECOGNIZE THAT VOICE?

HELLO, FRIENDS! IT'S THRILLING TO SEE YOU HERE!

FRUSH

PROFESSOR VON VOLT!

WE FINALLY FOUND YOU!

I KNEW I COULD COUNT ON YOU!

WE WOULDN'T LET YOU DOWN!

BUT WHAT ARE YOU DOING HIDING IN THE FLOWERS?

I WAS AFRAID THE CATS WOULD CHASE AFTER ME, SO I HID AND...

UH-OH! IT'S IMPOSSIBLE TO RELAX AROUND HERE!

GGGGRRRR....

HELPPPPP!

QUICK, RUN TO THE SPEEDRAT!

MEANWHILE, NOT TOO FAR AWAY, KAREN, BENJAMIN, AND BUGSY HAD ALSO...

QUICK, KIDS! WE'LL BE SAFE IN THE TALL PALM TREES!

AAHHHH!

...RUN INTO A PREHISTORIC ANIMAL!

WHAT KIND OF BEAST IS THAT?

IT'S AN OVIRAPTOR!

DOES THAT MEAN IT EATS EGGS?

NOT JUST EGGS! IT EATS A BIT OF ANYTHING IT FINDS!

OVIRAPTOR

ITS NAME MEANS "EGG THIEF," WHICH IS THE FOOD IT ATE, ALONG WITH MEAT AND SOME PLANTS. IT LOOKED LIKE A BIG BIRD, WAS PARTIALLY COVERED WITH FEATHERS, AND HAD LARGE CLAWS ON ITS FEET. IT HAD NO TEETH, A STRONG BEAK, AND A BONY CREST ON ITS HEAD. OVIRAPTORS WERE 8.2 FEET LONG AND WEIGHED AROUND 88 POUNDS.

LOOK! THOSE EGGS IN THE NEST ARE ATTRACTING IT!

IT'S GOING TO MAKE AN OMELET OUT OF THEM!

BUT FIRST IT'LL HAVE TO DO SOMETHING ABOUT THE DINOSAUR THAT JUST GOT HERE!

LOOK AT THOSE TEETH!!

IT'S FRIGHTENING!

IT'S A TYRANNO-SAURUS REX!

GRRRRRRR

ONE OF THE BIGGEST AND MOST FEROCIOUS CARNIVORES THAT EVER LIVED ON EARTH!

TYRANNOSAURUS REX

BETTER KNOWN BY ITS NICKNAME, T-REX, THIS DINOSAUR IS ONE OF THE LARGEST CARNIVORES THAT EVER LIVED ON EARTH. ITS NAME MEANS "TYRANT LIZARD," BECAUSE IT WAS THE UNOPPOSED RULER OF ITS TERRITORY. IT COULD REACH A LENGTH OF ALMOST 45 FEET AND WEIGHED ABOUT THE SAME AS TWO ELEPHANTS.

ROARRR

HA, HA! THE EGG THIEF IS RUNNING OFF!

NO ONE HAS THE COURAGE TO FACE A T-REX!

LET'S GET AWAY FROM HERE BEFORE THE TYRANNOSAURUS SEES US!

HEY! THERE'S SOMETHING OUT THERE IN THE MIDDLE OF THE SEA!

YOU'RE RIGHT! ANOTHER **CHASE!**

?!?

IT'S THE CATS! BUT THEY'RE NOT ALONE!

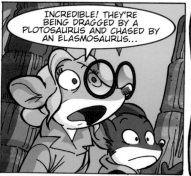

INCREDIBLE! THEY'RE BEING DRAGGED BY A PLOTOSAURUS AND CHASED BY AN ELASMOSAURUS...

ELASMOSAURUS

THE NAME OF THIS AQUATIC REPTILE, WHICH MEANS "RIBBON LIZARD," COMES FROM ITS NECK, WHICH COULD EXCEED 22 FEET IN LENGTH. BECAUSE OF ITS FLIPPERS, IT WAS ABLE TO MOVE WITH GREAT AGILITY AND CATCH FISH AND CRUSTACEANS, AND IT COULD ALSO EMERGE FROM THE WATER SUDDENLY TO CATCH FLYING REPTILES THAT GOT NEAR THE SURFACE.

THEY'RE HEADED RIGHT FOR THE **CORAL REEF!**

WATCH YOUR TAIL, BONZO! WE'VE GOT GUESTS!

OW, OW! AND WHO INVITED HIM?

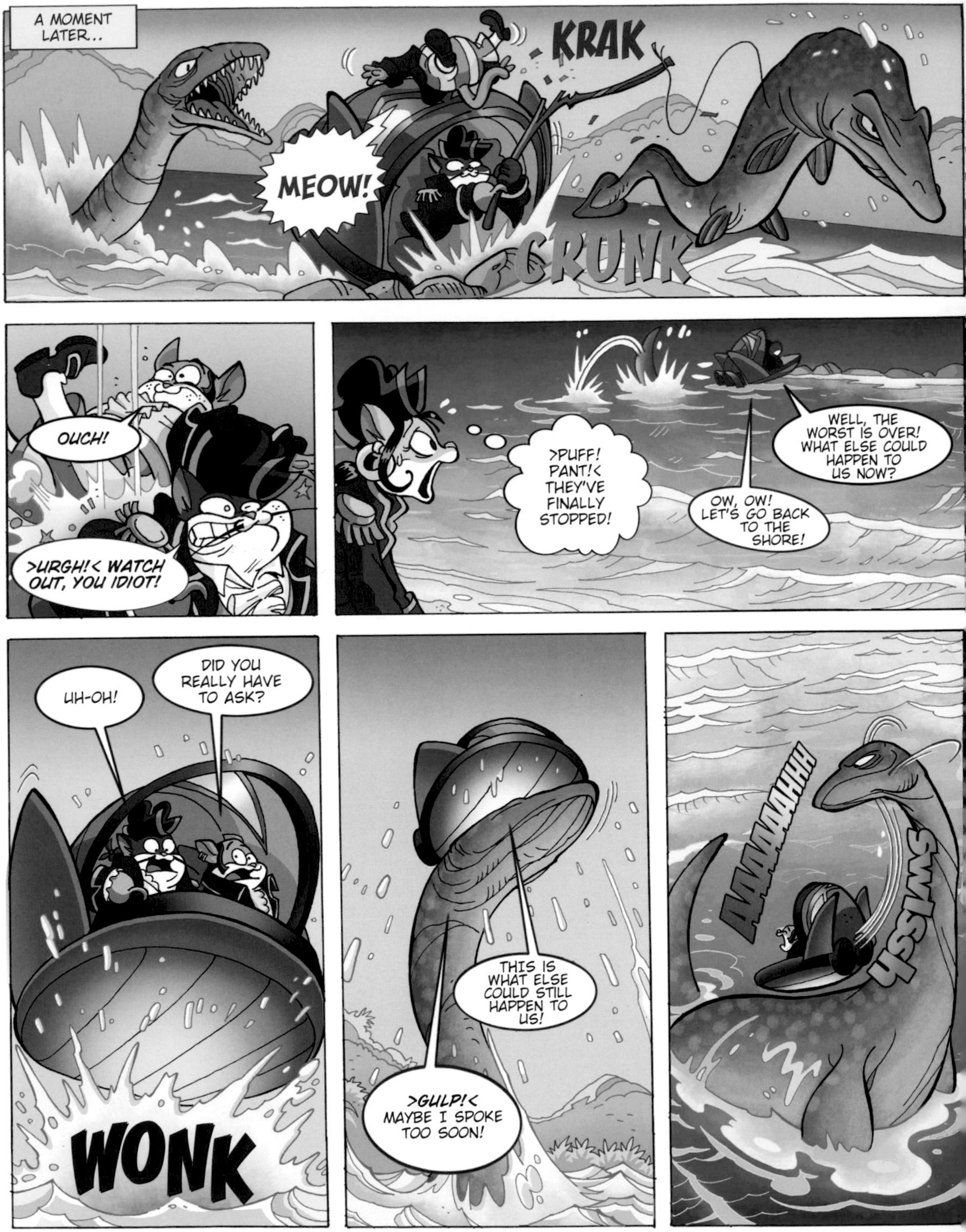

A MOMENT LATER...
KRAK
MEOW!
CRUNK
OUCH!
>URGH!< WATCH OUT, YOU IDIOT!
>PUFF! PANT!< THEY'VE FINALLY STOPPED!
WELL, THE WORST IS OVER! WHAT ELSE COULD HAPPEN TO US NOW?
OW, OW! LET'S GO BACK TO THE SHORE!
UH-OH!
DID YOU REALLY HAVE TO ASK?
WONK
THIS IS WHAT ELSE COULD STILL HAPPEN TO US!
>GULP!< MAYBE I SPOKE TOO SOON!
AAAAAHHH
SWISSH

DO YOU HAVE SOMETHING FOR **AIR SICKNESS?**

AIR SICKNESS? WHATEVER FOR? WE'RE IN THE SEA!

YES, BUT WE'RE TAKING OFF!

SMAK

WATCH OUT!

OW! OUCH!

BLONG

SO YOU DECIDED TO COME BACK AFTER ALL!

COME ON... WHAT HAPPENED TO YOUR **FISH?**

OW, OW! FISHY PUFFS ARE BETTER!

HEE, HEE! DID YOU LOSE YOUR APPETITE, PERHAPS?

AND HOW! I WANT TO GO HOME!

FIRST WE HAVE TO FIX THE CATJET! OR WE'LL BE STUCK HERE, TOO, JUST LIKE PROFESSOR VON VOLT!

QUICK, TO THE SPEEDRAT!

DID YOU HEAR? WE HAVE TO LET TRAP AND UNCLE G KNOW!

SHORTLY...

HERE'S THE SPEEDRAT!

BUT NO ONE'S HERE YET!

RELAX! YOU'LL SEE: THEY WON'T TAKE LONG TO ARRIV...

AAAAHHHHH

FRUSH!

TRAP... UNCLE G...

PROFESSOR VON VOLT!

RUN!!!

MAKE WAY!

FLUMMP

>SQUEEEAK!<

SBAM

HELP! THIS ONE HERE LOOKS HUNGRY!

>GULP!<

BLEAH! WHAT'S IT DOING?

MAYBE IT WANTS TO TASTE US FIRST!

SLURP

HA, HA! DON'T BE AFRAID! IT WON'T EAT YOU! THAT'S AN ANKYLOSAURUS!

A... WHAT?

BUT... IS IT REALLY SAFE?

OF COURSE! THIS DINOSAUR'S AN **HERBIVORE!**

ANKYLOSAURUS

THIS HERBIVOROUS DINOSAUR WAS UP TO 26 FEET LONG AND WEIGHED AS MUCH AS 7 TONS. ITS BODY WAS PROTECTED BY THICK BONY ARMOR MADE UP OF PLATES THAT ALSO HAD SPINES ON THEM. ON ITS MUZZLE WERE TWO PAIRS OF SPINES TO PROTECT IT, ONE ON ITS HEAD AND ANOTHER EVEN WITH ITS JAW. IN ADDITION, ANKYLOSAURS HAD A LONG TAIL WITH A SORT OF CLUB AT THE END, WHICH IT USED TO DEFEND ITSELF FROM ATTACKERS.

OKAY, BUT TELL IT TO CUT IT OUT! IT'S GOT ME CONFUSED WITH A **LOLLIPOP!**

PLFF

THAT'S BECAUSE YOU'RE COVERED WITH GINKGO BILOBA SEEDS! THE HERBIVORES ARE CRAZY ABOUT THEM!

SO IT FOLLOWED US BECAUSE IT SMELLED THE SCENT OF THE SEEDS!

OH! SO THAT'S WHAT THAT STICKY JAM WAS!

GINKGO BILOBA

CHARLES DARWIN CALLED THE GINKGO BILOBA A LIVING FOSSIL. ACTUALLY, IT'S THE ONLY PLANT FROM THE DINOSAUR AGE (IT APPEARED IN THE JURASSIC) TO SURVIVE AND REACH OUR TIME WITHOUT SUBSTANTIAL CHANGES. THE LEAVES OF THE PLANT HAVE THE CHARACTERISTIC SHAPE OF AN OPEN FAN, AND THE TREE PRODUCES SEEDS SURROUNDED BY A PULPY COVERING.

IT'S TRUE! LOOK, MORE OF THEM ARE COMING!

>HEE, HEE!< THE GINKGO BILOBA MUST TASTE GOOD TO THEM!

HA, HA! LOOK AT THAT FUNNY-LOOKING THING COVERED WITH **FEATHERS!**

AARGH! A VELOCIRAPTOR!

!!!

WE'LL BE SAFE IN THE TREES!

THEY'RE TOO FAR... THE VELOCIRAPTOR WOULD GET TO US FIRST!

WE THOUGHT WE WERE DONE FOR WHEN SOMETHING HAPPENED THAT I WILL NEVER FORGET...

...AND THAT ONCE AGAIN REMINDED ME HOW IMPORTANT IT IS TO FACE DIFFICULTIES AND CONFRONT ADVERSITY TOGETHER!

UH-OH! THEY'RE ATTACKING US!

THUMP

THE ANKYLOSAURS DEFENDED US AND THEMSELVES FROM DANGER BY USING THEIR STRENGTH TO HELP THE HERD...

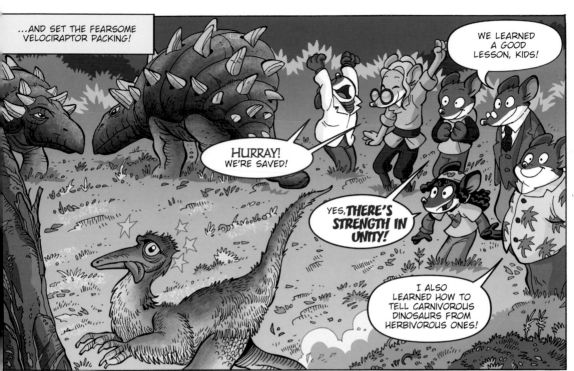

...AND SET THE FEARSOME VELOCIRAPTOR PACKING!

WE LEARNED A GOOD LESSON, KIDS!

HURRAY! WE'RE SAVED!

YES, **THERE'S STRENGTH IN UNITY!**

I ALSO LEARNED HOW TO TELL CARNIVOROUS DINOSAURS FROM HERBIVOROUS ONES!

IT'S EASY! IF I MEET A DINOSAUR THAT TRIES TO EAT ME... THAT MEANS IT'S A CARNIVORE!

BUT IF IT WOULD RATHER LICK ME... THEN I DEFINITELY LIKE IT BETTER!

THAT'S AN ORIGINAL POINT OF VIEW, RIGHT, DOCTOR?

HA HA HA HA HE HE

PALEONTOLOGISTS USUALLY USE OTHER CRITERIA TO CLASSIFY DINOSAURS!

WELL, I'M ALL FOR SIMPLE EXPLANATIONS!

THE DIFFERENCE BETWEEN SAURISCHIAN AND ORNITHISCHIAN DINOSAURS

DINOSAURS ARE REPTILES OF VARIOUS SIZES. THEY CAN BE SEPARATED INTO TWO MAIN GROUPS: SAURISCHIANS AND ORNITHISCHIANS. THE DISTINCTION BETWEEN THESE TWO IS BASED ON THE DIFFERENT STRUCTURE OF THEIR PELVIC BONES: ORNITHISCHIANS, WHICH ARE CHARACTERIZED BY A PELVIS THAT TURNS TOWARDS THE BACK, LIKE TODAY'S BIRDS, WERE ALL HERBIVORES; THE SAURISCHIANS, INSTEAD, WERE CHARACTERIZED BY A PELVIS THAT TURNED TOWARDS THE FRONT, LIKE TODAY'S REPTILES, AND WERE MOSTLY CARNIVORES.

43

THE SUN WAS SETTING BY NOW. THIS WAS THE SAME SUN THAT MILLIONS OF YEARS LATER WOULD BE LIGHTING OUR DAYS ON MOUSE ISLAND. THAT DAY OUR SURPRISES...

...WEREN'T OVER YET!

MOLDY MOZZARELLA! LOOK UP THERE!

IT'S THE *CATJET!*

YES, THE FOOTSTEPS WE FOLLOWED ALONG THE BEACH WERE THOSE OF THE PIRATE CATS!

WHEN WE SAW THEM, WE IMMEDIATELY RAN TO LET YOU KNOW, BUT IT WAS TOO LATE. THEY WERE ALREADY RUSHING OFF!

RIGHT! THOSE RASCALS HAVE GIVEN US THE SLIP AGAIN!

BUT AT LEAST YOU RESCUED ME, MY FRIENDS. THANK YOU VERY MUCH!

THEY DON'T KNOW YOU CAME HERE... THEY THINK THEY'VE ABANDONED ME IN THE CRETACEOUS PERIOD!

BUT WE KNOW JUST WHERE TO FIND THEM: AT THE MOUSE ISLAND HARBOR!

THAT'S WHERE THEY TOOK ME AFTER THEY KIDNAPPED ME! THE CATS' SHIP WAS DOCKED AT THE PIER!

SO IT'LL BE EASY TO FIND THEM! LET'S NOT WASTE ANY MORE TIME!

LET'S GO!

MOUSE ISLAND, HERE WE COME!

AS WE WERE LEAVING, I NOTICED A LOOK OF LONGING IN KAREN VON FOSSILS'S EYES...

DON'T BE **SAD**, DR. VON FOSSILS!

NO, I'M JUST DEEPLY MOVED. THANKS TO YOU, I'VE HAD AN UNFORGETTABLE EXPERIENCE.

I THINK THAT TRICERATOPS CAME TO TELL US GOODBYE!

HOW SWEET! SEEING IT GIVES ME AN IDEA!

IN NO TIME AT ALL, PROF. VON VOLT. PROGRAMMED THE SPEEDRAT TO TAKE US BACK TO MOUSE ISLAND...

HOLD ON TIGHT... WE'RE LEAVING!

TAP TAP
TAP TAP

...AND WE SOON ARRIVED AT THE MOUSE ISLAND HARBOR, WHERE THE CATS WERE GETTING READY TO LEAVE AGAIN!

♪♫

MANY ARE WE! WICKED WE BE! WRECKING AND ROBBING ALL SHIPS IN THE SEA!

THERE THEY ARE! THEY HAVEN'T SEEN US!

>BRRR!< THAT SONG GIVES ME THE WILLIES!

YOU'LL SHAKE AND YOU'LL SHIVER FROM PIRATE CATS THREE!

REMEMBER THE LESSON WE LEARNED: THERE'S STRENGTH IN UNITY! THAT'S THE ONLY WAY WE CAN DEFEAT THEM!

HEAVE-HO!

>OOF!< IT'S SO HEAVY!

GET CRACKING! WE HAVE TO LEAVE BEFORE THE SUN RISES! NO ONE MUST SEE US!

HOW COME YOU'RE IN SUCH A HURRY?

>GULP!< BUT WHO...?

?!?

IT'S STILTON! AND HE'S GOT HIS FRIENDS WITH HIM!

LOOK WHO IT IS!

DID YOU COME TO KEEP US COMPANY?

WHAT'S GNAWING AT YOU, MOUSE? AREN'T YOU GLAD TO SEE US?

HEE, HEE, HEE!

WE'RE NOT DOING ANYTHING WRONG...

>HUMPH!< THIS ISN'T A COURTESY CALL!

PROF. VON VOLT DOESN'T AGREE!

LIARS!

>TSK!< YOUR NOSY PARKER FRIEND! WE'VE GOT HIM OUT OF THE WAY NOW! HE'S SOMEWHERE WHERE HE'LL HAVE LOTS OF FUN!

AND NOW YOU'LL MEET THE SAME END!

RIGHT! DON'T LET US INTIMIDATE YOU TWO RODENTS!

YOU COUNTED WRONG... IT'S NOT JUST THESE TWO!

BUT... HOW IS THIS POSSIBLE?!?

>GULP!<

PROFESSOR VON VOLT!

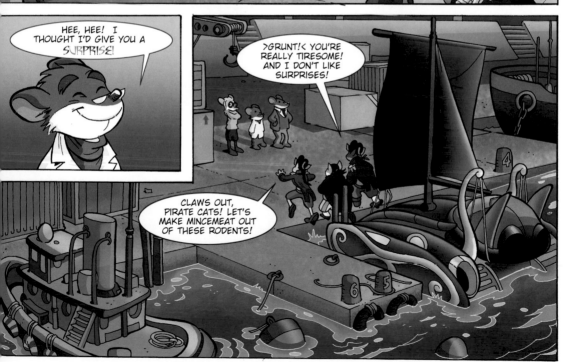

HEE, HEE! I THOUGHT I'D GIVE YOU A SURPRISE!

>GRUNT!< YOU'RE REALLY TIRESOME! AND I DON'T LIKE SURPRISES!

CLAWS OUT, PIRATE CATS! LET'S MAKE MINCEMEAT OUT OF THESE RODENTS!

MAYBE I DIDN'T EXPLAIN MYSELF PROPERLY! THE SURPRISE WE ARRANGED IS SOMETHING ELSE!

WE BROUGHT SOMEONE WITH US WHO'S ANXIOUS TO MEET YOU!

HERE HE IS! HIS NAME IS TRICERARAT!

GGRRRAAARRRGH!!!

I'M OUTTA HERE! I'VE HAD ENOUGH OF THESE MEETINGS ALREADY!

>GASP!< A DINOSAUR!!

LET'S GET OUTTA HERE! EVERY CAT FOR THEMSELVES!

GRRRRRR

DON'T YOU HAVE TO TEACH US A LESSON?

SOME OTHER TIME...

WHERE ARE YOU RUSHING OFF TO?

...WITHOUT A DINOSAUR AROUND!

LOOK AT THEM RUN AWAY!

DID YOU LIKE OUR PERFORM-ANCE?

IT WAS PERFECT, KIDS!

I EVEN WAS ALMOST AFRAID, MYSELF, WHEN I SAW YOU SUDDENLY JUMP OUT!

YOU? AFRAID? WHAT ELSE IS NEW!

HA, HA, HA!

THAT COSTUME WAS A GREAT IDEA!

IN THE **DARK**, IT LOOKED LIKE A REAL DINOSAUR!

THE DARKNESS PLAYED IN OUR FAVOR!

AH... MORNING...

WE WERE JUST IN TIME. NOW IT'S MORNING!

...IS MY FAVORITE TIME BECAUSE THAT'S WHEN WE EAT BREAKFAST!

BY THE WAY, WHAT WOULD YOU SAY TO... TREATING ME TO BREAKFAST?

HURRAY! BREAKFAST FOR EVERYBODY!

WELL, AFTER AN ADVENTURE LIKE THIS, YOU DESERVE IT!

AFTERNOON IS MY SECOND FAVORITE TIME OF THE DAY, BECAUSE THEN WE HAVE... LUNCH TIME!

RAT-TASTIC! LET'S GET TOGETHER AGAIN THIS AFTERNOON!

MY DEAR RODENT FRIENDS, FAREWELL UNTIL THE NEXT TIME... ANOTHER WHISKERFUL OF AN ADVENTURE, WRITTEN BY STILTON... *Geronimo Stilton!*

HA, HA!

Watch Out For
PAPERCUTZ

One of the many questions editors "What exactly do editors actually do?" Well, in my case, it's to remember to introduce myself here on the *Watch Out for Papercutz* page. Hi, I'm Salicrup, Jim Salicrup, and I'm the Editor-in-Chief of Papercutz. And for those of you not familiar with Papercutz, Papercutz is dedicated to publishing great graphic novels for all ages—such as Geronimo Stilton.

I'll be the first to admit that my life isn't a fraction as interesting as the world-famous editor of *The Rodent's Gazette*, Geronimo Stilton. I can't remember when I ever had to travel back in time to prevent the Pirate Cats from tampering with history. Although I have edited such comics as *Doctor Who* and *The Time-Bandits* over the years—and that might've helped prepare me for GERONIMO STILTON.

You'd be surprised about what exactly does get us all worked up here at the Papercutz editorial offices. For example, our good friend Ortho, the letterer on our GERONIMO STILTON graphic novels, was commenting on how Geronimo Stilton's name came from the famous Native American, Geronimo. Associate Editor Michael Petranek didn't quite see things that way, informing us all that the name Geronimo is just a variation of the name Jerome (or Latin for Hieronymus, if you go back far enough). Well, that's when the sparks started to fly! Ortho insisted that that wasn't true. That the name was created when the Mexicans dubbed a young Apache warrior, "Geronimo."

While Michael and Ortho were arguing, that's when I started Googling "Geronimo." One of the most interesting stories was found in Wikipedia:

The alleged finding of human remains, designated San Geronimo, in 1853 afforded striking confirmation of an incident recorded by a Spanish Benedictine named Diego de Haëdo, who published a topography of Algeria in 1612. Haëdo sets forth the legend that a young Arab who had embraced Christianity, and had been baptized with the name of Geronimo, had been captured by a Moorish corsair in 1569 and taken to Algiers. The Arabs endeavored to induce Geronimo to renounce Christianity, but as he steadfastly refused to do so, he was condemned to death. Bound hand and foot, he was thrown alive into a mould in which a block of concrete was about to be made. The block containing his body was built into an angle of the Fort of the Twenty-four Hours, then under construction. According to Samuel M. Zwemer (see link below), in 1853 the Fort of the Twenty-four Hours was demolished, and in the very angle specified by Haedo the skeleton of Geronimo was found. The bones were interred at St. Philippe. Liquid plaster of Paris was run into the mould left by the saint's body, creating a perfect model showing the features of the youth, the cords which bound him, and even the texture of his clothing. This model was said to be held in the museum formerly at Parc du Galland, Mustapha Superior, Algiers.

Wow! Who knew? Then there's also an interesting theory on why paratroopers yell "Geronimo!" when they leap out of plane, but we'll have to save that for next time, as we're almost out of room! And one of the main things all editors know how to do, is to cut long stories short! So, be here next time, when Geronimo Stilton again saves the future, by protecting the past!

Thanks, *Jim*

Who doesn't love pirates? You know, the fictional kind that say "Yaarr" and "Shiver me timbers" all the time. Papercutz Associate Editor Michael Petranek recalls that when he was a kid, he'd pick up a stick, pretend it was his sword, and join his friends aboard an abandoned 10-foot boat that they discovered in an alley in Dallas, Texas. "We weren't just playing pirates," Michael says, "We were pirates!" With the success of the Pirates of the Caribbean, featuring Johnny Depp's Captain Jack Sparrow, there seems to be no end in sight to our fascination with these nautical nasties. We thought it might be fun to take a look at the pirates that have made their way from their poopdecks and onto the pages of your favorite graphic novels. So, avast ye swabs, and gather about to hear the hoary tale of...

THE PIRATES OF PAPERCUTZ ™

Much of what we think of as pirates today all began in Robert Louis Stevenson's immensely popular 1882 novel "Treasure Island,' which is faithfully adapted into comics by David Chauvel and Fred Simon in CLASSICS ILLUSTRATED DELUXE #4. The story is about young Jim Hawkins and his adventures after he encounters legendary pirate Long John Silver. All the elements are here—there's a mutiny, a hunt for buried treasure, and much, much more. Here's just a brief taste of what to expect—after Long John Silver arrives on the island where they expect to find buried treasure, he betrays Dr. Livesey who helped bring him to the island. Under a white flag, Silver enters the stockade Livesey and his men are holed up at, to offer a dubious truce. Negotiations don't go well, and as seemingly diplomatic Long John Silver leaves, he reveals a bit of his true colors...

THERE! THAT'S WHAT I THINK OF YE!

BEFORE AN HOUR'S OUT, I'LL STOVE IN YOUR OLD BLOCKHOUSE LIKE A RUM PUNCHEON! LAUGH, BY THUNDER! YE'LL SOON LAUGH UPON THE OTHER SIDE.

PFFT

THEM THAT DIE'LL BE THE LUCKY ONES!

AND WITH A DREADFUL OATH HE STUMBLED OFF.

CLASSICS ILLUSTRATED DELUXE #5 "Treasure Island" not only tells an epic adventure story with dramatic battles and nail-biting moments of suspense, it also established much of what is considered pirate lore today. A few examples…

The Black Spot: A message of impending doom given from one pirate to another.

HE HAD TILL TEN, MOTHER.

You have till ten tonight.

PIECES OF EIGHT!
PIECES OF EIGHT!

NOW, THAT BIRD IS MAYBE TWO HUNDRED YEARS OLD, HAWKINS. SHE'S SAILED WITH ENGLAND THE PIRATE. SHE'S BEEN AT MADAGASCAR, AND AT MALABAR, AND SURINAM, AND PROVIDENCE, AND PORTOBELLO.

AH, SHE'S A HANDSOME CRAFT, SHE IS.

THE BIRD WOULD PECK AT THE BARS AND SWEAR STRAIGHT ON, PASSING BELIEF FOR WICKEDNESS.

THERE, YOU CAN'T TOUCH PITCH AND NOT BE MUCKED, LAD. THIS POOR OLD INNOCENT BIRD O' MIN[swearing blue fire and none the wiser

Parrots on the Shoulders of Pirates:
Long John Silver named his parrot "Captain Flint."

X Marks the Spot:
The dark origins of the phrase "X marks the spot" come from the British navy. When they put someone in front of a firing squad, a piece of paper with an X on it was placed upon the person who was to be executed, to provide soldiers a clear target. Treasure maps in comics and movies almost always have an "X" that marks the spot where treasure has been buried. This appears in "Treasure Island" in the form of a map that Dr. Livesey finds…

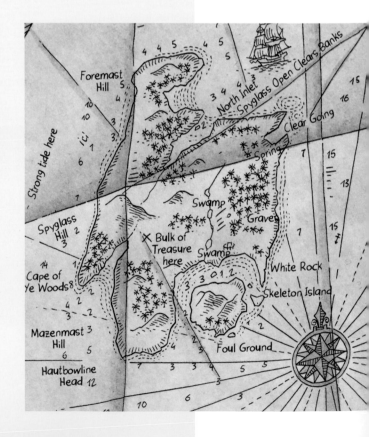

Robert Louis Stevenson's pirates in "Treasure Island" became the model for virtually all fictional pirates to follow. J.M. Barrie's 1904 fantasy-filled play Peter Pan, or, The Boy Who Wouldn't Grow Up contributed Captain Hook, a pirate who "was Blackbeard's boatswain, and… the only man Long John Silver ever feared" to the pantheon of pernicious pirates. Yet, Hook's right hand was cut off by Peter Pan and swallowed by a crocodile, which is why Hook seeks revenge on Peter. Tinker Bell, Peter's feisty fairy friend was also introduced in that play, which soon became a novel, and was the inspiration for the classic Disney animated film Peter Pan.

The DISNEY FAIRIES graphic novels have mainly focused on the adventures of Tinker Bell, and her fellow fairies Prilla, Beck, Rani, and Vidia, among others, in Pixie Hollow in Never Land. Captain Hook makes his long-awaited comics appearance in DISNEY FAIRIES graphic novel #4 "Tinker Bell to the Rescue":

In his DISNEY FAIRIES appearances, Captain Hook may not be as fearsome as Long John Silver, but he still has a lot in common with Silver. Most obviously, he is also missing a limb! The biggest difference is that Silver's adventures are more or less set in the real world, while Hook literally resides in Never Land. And do you know how to get to Never Land? It's easy! You just head toward the second star on your right and fly straight on till morning, you'll come to Never Land. It's the flying part that's a little tricky.

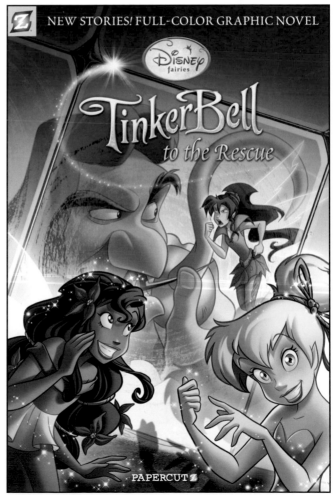

Just as exciting and exotic as Treasure Island and Never Land is New Mouse City, which, as we're sure you already know is where Geronimo Stilton lives. Geronimo is the famous editor of The Rodent's Gazette, and quite an adventurer himself. When not editing the great mousetropolitan newspaper, Geronimo is travelling through time to prevent the meddlesome Pirate Cats from changing history. Yes, Pirate Cats. Catardone III of Catatonia is the ruler of the Pirate Cats, and his dream is to become the richest and most famous cat of all time. His daughter, Tersilla of Catatonia, may be the real brains behind the Pirate Cats. And Bonzo Felix is Catardone's assistant. Take a look at the Bonzo and Felix as seen in GERONIMO STILTON graphic novel #6 "Who Stole the Mona Lisa?" Notice anything in particular?

While both cats share Long John Silver's fashion sense, Catardone also has a hook, instead of a hand—or is that a paw? Aside from being cats that walk upright and speak, these Pirate Cats can also travel through time in their catjet. While neither Long John Silver nor Captain Hook have ever been particularly successful, the Pirate Cats are even more incompetent. These pirates would much rather get their paws on a plate of fresh fish than a treasure chest. Yet, it would be a big mistake to think that they're pushovers. They always manage to get away to fight another day. After all, like most cats, they're always able to land on their feet.

Whether in the pages of CLASSICS ILLUSTRATED DELUXE, DISNEY FAIRIES, or GERONIMO STILTON, one thing is certain, we haven't seen the last of the pirates of Papercutz! Yaarr! 𝓏

THE PIRATE CATS TRAVEL TO THE PAST ON THE CATJET SO THAT THEY CAN CHANGE HISTORY AND BECOME RICH AND FAMOUS. BUT GERONIMO AND THE STILTON FAMILY ALWAYS MANAGE TO UNMASK THEM!

CATJET